MORAX THE WRECKING MENACE

BY ADAM BLADE

ORCHARD

With special thanks to Tabitha Jones

For William Richards and David and Isabella Stobie

www.beastquest.co.uk

ORCHARD BOOKS

First published in Great Britain in 2020 by The Watts Publishing Group

1 3 5 7 9 10 8 6 4 2

A CIP catalogue record for this book is available from the British Library.

ISBN 978 1 40835 779 8

Printed in Great Britain

The paper and board used in this book are made from wood from responsible sources

Orchard Books
An imprint of Hachette Children's Group
Part of The Watts Publishing Group Limited
Carmelite House, 50 Victoria Embankment, London EC4Y 0DZ

An Hachette UK Company
www.hachette.co.uk
www.hachettechildrens.co.uk

Welcome to the world of Beast Quest!

Tom was once an ordinary village boy, until he travelled to the City, met King Hugo and discovered his destiny. Now he is the Master of the Beasts, sworn to defend Avantia and its people against Evil. Tom draws on the might of the magical Golden Armour, and is protected by powerful tokens granted to him by the Good Beasts of Avantia. Tom and his loyal companion Elenna are always ready to visit new lands and tackle the enemies of the realm.

While there's blood in his veins, Tom will never give up the Quest...

GREAT
PALACE OF
PYLORIS
DANGER
FOREST

PYLORIS
STORM PYRAMID
DESTINY
BONE SANDS
BURIED CITY
UNDERGROUND LAKE

There are special gold coins to collect in this book. You will earn one coin for every chapter you read.

Find out what to do with your coins at the end of the book.

CONTENTS

Banners fly from the walls of King Hugo's Palace and all Avantia rejoices at Tom's latest victory. The people worship the snivelling wretch as if he's their saviour.

Well, forgive me if I'm not bowing down. He killed my father Sanpao and drove my mother Kensa from the kingdom.

So, in revenge, I'm going to spoil their little party.

Soon Avantia will face a Beast like no other.

And when they look for their little hero to save their skins, he will be nowhere to be found.

Ria

BENEATH THE DESERT

Elenna scrambled to her feet, sending a cascade of rubble sliding from her back. Daltec let out a groan as he heaved himself out of the debris to stand on the island of rock beside her. Golden evening light slanted down through a gap in the cave roof far above, piercing the

clouds of dust hanging in the gloom. But it didn't reach the dark surface of the lake that filled the cavern – until recently the home of a tentacled underwater Beast called Fluger. Elenna peered anxiously up through the hole but couldn't see any sign of Tom and Ria. And she couldn't hear wingbeats either. Her stomach churned with worry. *We have to catch them!* After taking a token from the defeated Beast, Tom and Ria had escaped on the back of Ria's flying horse, bringing down the ceiling as they went…right on top of Elenna and Daltec.

"Are you all right?" Elenna asked Daltec as he brushed chips of stone from his robe. A gash on his forehead showed where a rock had struck him, but his eyes looked clear.

"Just bruised," Daltec said. Then he let out a heavy sigh. "But now the vial with the antidote to Ria's enchantment is broken, how can we hope to cure Tom?"

Elenna's heart clenched with anguish at the memory of Tom scowling down at her from the back of Ria's winged stallion. He hadn't seemed to care at all that Ria had tried to bury his friends alive. *It's not his fault,* Elenna reminded herself. Ria had enchanted Tom's Golden Armour, turning it black and changing its power from Good to Evil. Under its influence, Tom was Ria's slave. Elenna had hoped to cure him with a potion. *But now the potion is gone, and Ria and Tom could be anywhere…* She took a deep breath and squared her shoulders. "We haven't followed Tom all the way to the Kingdom of Pyloris just to give up on him now," she said. "We'll find him. And when we do, I'll drag him through the portal back to Avantia if I have to. But we need to get out of here first."

Elenna heard the scuff of hooves from above and looked up to see Storm's head appear over the edge of the hole in the ceiling. The stallion's movements dislodged more rubble, sending it plunging into the lake. He gave a startled whicker and skittered back out of sight.

"We can escape using my magic," Daltec said, but then he frowned down at Elenna's sodden clothes. "Let me dry you off first." Elenna clenched her teeth to stifle a shiver, only now realising how cold she felt.

As Daltec lifted his hands, his palms began to glow with a soft golden light. He made a sweeping gesture towards Elenna, casting the light over her like a net. She felt a sudden rush of warmth, and steam rose from her soaked tunic. But the sensation quickly faded, leaving her almost as drenched as before.

Daltec grimaced. "Well... That didn't work as well as I had expected," he said.

"I'll dry off quickly enough once

we're out of here," Elenna said. "Let's go."

Daltec closed his eyes and drew a deep breath, then let it out slowly, moving his hands in a wide circle, ending with an upward thrust. Elenna's heart gave a skip as her feet left the rock and she drifted upwards. Daltec began to float too, his eyes still closed, and his palms facing the ceiling, but then he gave a startled yelp. Elenna's stomach flipped as they both tumbled back down. She landed in a crouch while Daltec crashed down beside her in a pile of limbs and tangled cloak.

Elenna helped the young wizard to his feet.

"Thank you," he said. Then he looked down at his hands, his brows pinched together with worry. He shook his head. "This isn't good," he said. "Something about this kingdom is interfering with my magic."

"Then let's hope Ria has the same problem," Elenna said. She peered across the lake at the shadowy cavern walls, looking for the easiest escape route. During their fight with Fluger, huge stalactites and chunks of stone had been dislodged from the ceiling. They poked up from the inky water like broken teeth. Elenna glanced at Daltec in his long flowing robe. "It'll be too dangerous for you to climb out," she said. "I'll go first, then send a rope down for you." Balancing lightly on the balls of her feet, Elenna leapt from rock to rock, making her way steadily through the gloom. Once she reached the craggy cavern wall, she scaled it easily. *Now for the tricky bit*, she thought, looking at the wide stretch of overhanging ceiling she needed to cover to reach the opening.

She took a deep breath and hooked the fingers of one hand into a crack in the roof, then the other. Stalactites still dotted the ceiling, but Elenna had seen too many fall to trust them with her weight. Instead, she lifted both feet and, wedging her heels, toes and fingers into nooks and crannies in the rock, clambered backwards across the ceiling. The climb strained every part of her body, and by the time she reached the opening, her stomach muscles burned and her arms trembled.

With the last of her strength, she heaved herself up into the open and collapsed on the rocky ground. Storm bent over her, blowing warm breath into her face.

"Hello," Elenna said, smiling and stroking his cheek. Then she pulled herself up, shook out her aching fingers and rummaged in the horse's saddlebag for a rope.

Tying one end around the pommel of Storm's saddle, Elenna crossed to the rocky opening in the desert floor and peered down at Daltec.

"Catch!" she said, throwing the end of the rope. Daltec snatched it from the air, knotted it around his chest, then held tight.

"Ready!" he called up.

Elenna led Storm away from the hole, dragging Daltec up behind them.

After a few moments, Daltec called for her to stop.

"Whoa, Storm," she called out. Instantly, the stallion became still. Elenna returned to the hole to see the wizard dangling just below the rim. She reached out a hand for his, then, bracing her feet, pulled with all her strength while he heaved himself over the lip. Daltec fell to his knees, red-faced and sweating and looked up at Elenna with a sheepish smile.

"That must be the most undignified escape any wizard has

made in the history of Avantia!" he said.

Elenna grinned. "I won't tell if you won't." But as she gazed about the wide expanse of desert, her smile faded, and a cold, sick feeling settled in her stomach. "Why do you think Ria's doing all this?" she asked. "She's already collected two tokens from the ancient Beasts that Tanner split Krokol into, and I'm guessing she's after the third. But why?"

"I wish I knew," Daltec said, untying the rope from his chest. "All I can say is that her plan is sure to be evil."

"And she doesn't care who she hurts on the way," Elenna said.

"We have to rescue Tom before it's too late. His heart is still good – I can feel it. Deep inside, he must be fighting the enchantment."

Daltec shook his head sadly. "We can only hope his true nature can withstand Ria's spell," he said. Daltec drew Tom's magic compass from his cloak and held it level in his hand. He had replaced the needle with a fragment of the helmet of Tom's blackened armour, left behind in Avantia. It would show which way Tom and Ria had gone.

Elenna watched the needle swing back and forth, eventually settling to point towards the red disc of the sun sitting low on the western horizon.

"Let's go," she said, swinging up on to Storm's back. Daltec climbed up behind her. She pressed her heels into the stallion's side, and he started off at a quick trot over the desert sand.

We're coming, Tom! Elenna thought. *While there's blood in my veins, I won't fail you.*

1

DESERT OASIS

Seated behind Ria on her flying stallion, Tom gazed down at the seemingly endless desert, now stained a dull and shadowy red in the light of the setting sun.

"What are we doing here, anyway?" he asked Ria. "Those two tokens you're hanging on to must be good for something – otherwise, why would you spend so long in this horrible wasteland? What's your plan?"

"None of your business," Ria snapped. "Frankly, I'm starting to wonder why I bothered bringing you along at all. You're supposed to be Master of the Beasts, but you almost got yourself killed by Fluger. And Electro before that. If Elenna wasn't following you around, coming to your rescue, you'd be long dead. Is that how it always is on your Beast Quests – Elenna saving you all the time?"

"Of course not!" Tom snapped, feeling a hot rush of shame, and hung his head. Then he muttered, "I won't let you down again."

"You'd better not," Ria said. "We're about to face the last of Krokol's three Beasts. He's the deadliest yet. And we've almost reached his territory. Look." Ria pointed ahead.

In the distance, Tom could see the jagged outline of a huge dark fissure in the desert floor surrounded by what looked like stunted bushes. As they drew close, he found the parched sands ended abruptly at the edge of a rocky valley, filled with dense, dark forest. *An oasis!*

Ria's winged stallion flew onwards, carrying them right above the trees. At first, the thick canopy hid the ground from sight. But soon, they passed over a clearing filled with jagged stumps and flattened vegetation. Tom frowned. *What kind of Beast could do that?* A tingle of fear traced his spine. But as his pulse quickened, he smiled and balled his fists. *Whatever it is, Ria wants it dead, so I'll defeat it!* As they flew on, Tom saw that more open areas, all filled with shattered trunks, dotted the forest.

Ria tugged at her horse's reins, angling the stallion down towards one of the clearings. They landed in a patch of ferns. Ria slid from her mount's back, and Tom leapt down

beside her. Broken tree trunks leaned against each other at crazy angles all around them. Tom peered into the dusky forest, looking for any sign of the Beast.

"Don't just stand there!" Ria snapped, striding off into the gloom. "You're on a Quest, remember?" Tom hurried to keep up with her, leaving the winged stallion to graze on the ferns.

A cold, cloying mist rose from the earth beneath the trees, quickly chilling Tom to the bone. The rich smell of decay filled the air, along with a musty animal stench that caught in Tom's throat. Hairy tendrils of grey-green moss hung down from the tree branches like shabby curtains, making it hard to see more than a few paces ahead. The dead air muffled the sound of their footsteps, and apart from the occasional croak of a frog, or the chirp of an insect, nothing stirred. Suddenly a twig snapped somewhere above them. Tom looked up, holding his breath in the silence. He couldn't see anything moving in amongst the dark leaves and stringy moss, but still, the hair on his arms prickled. He could feel eyes watching him. Another twig snapped. Leaves rustled in the canopy. Ria strode on, not even bothering to look back. Tom hurried to catch her up.

"You know there's something following us?" he hissed.

Ria nodded. "That's why I've brought you along. Protection."

Tom kept pace with Ria as she trudged onwards through the forest. As he peered back and forth into the shadows, his senses felt ultra-sharp, and his muscles were coiled tight, ready to attack. *Whatever's following us had better watch out!* Soon the hunger to fight became almost unbearable.

Tom stopped, his hand on the hilt of his sword. "So, where is this Beast, then?" he asked Ria. "I'm ready to give it a taste of my blade."

"Don't worry," Ria said. "You'll get your chance to show off. I'm sure the Beast will find us before long."

Tom let out a huff of irritation and was about to start off again. But then he heard another twig snap, louder than before and right behind him. He spun round. The green moss hanging from a nearby tree seemed to shift. Tom blinked, and with a sudden jolt, noticed shiny black eyes gazing back at him from a leathery, green face. *What in all Avantia...?* A greyish-green monkey about the size of a small man hung upside down from a branch. And, as Tom peered at it, the creature smiled, revealing huge yellow teeth.

"Ria!" Tom cried, just as she let out a startled yelp. Tom turned to see two more mangy-looking green monkeys hauling her up into the treetops.

"Let her go!" Tom shouted. But before he could draw his sword, a pair of strong hands seized his own upper arms, holding them fast.

With a stomach-churning lurch, he was whipped upwards through the leaves.

3

A CLOSE CALL

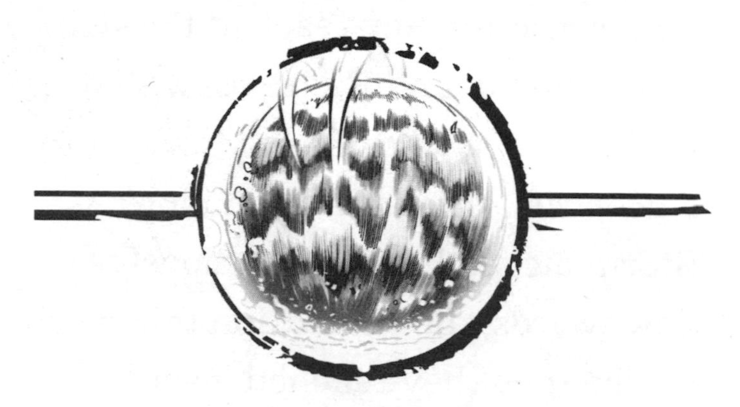

The low evening sun shone red in Elenna's eyes as Storm carried her and Daltec across the desert. With the heat of the day gone, her fingers felt stiff on the reins, and a sharp chill misted her breath. Suddenly, the stallion pricked his ears and quickened his pace. Gazing into the sunset, Elenna spotted what looked like a line of straggly bushes ahead silhouetted against the sky. *An oasis?*

Before long, they reached the strip of scrubland, and Elenna saw that the ground sloped sharply away into a deep rift, shrouded in shadow. As Storm picked his way cautiously downwards, the vegetation thickened. By the time they reached level ground, tall trees choked with vines and hanging moss surrounded them.

"Look!" Daltec said, suddenly, pointing to a broad tree trunk nearby. Elenna could see pale lines cut into the grey-green bark. The carving appeared to show a handful of stocky, bow-legged figures aiming spears and arrows at what seemed to be a huge boulder. Elenna frowned, trying to puzzle the scene out.

"That's strange," she said. "I can't imagine those weapons being much use against stone."

"No," Daltec said, leaning forwards to run a hand over the scored wood. "But this carving's recent, which means there may be a tribe living nearby. We should be wary."

They pressed onwards through the twilit jungle, coils of mist rising from the damp earth all around them. Elenna peered into the shadows, looking for any sign of the people who had made the carving – but the forest was eerily still. Storm soon slowed, thick mud sucking at his hooves, and as they pushed through a curtain of moss, the trees thinned suddenly. Elenna pulled the stallion to a halt. The ground dropped away before them into a steep-sided gully about the width of a well-travelled road. Boggy mud filled the ditch, and its slick sides oozed with water. The wide muddy trench ran right across their path and appeared to go on for a long way in each direction.

"It's almost dark," Daltec said. "And it's going to be tricky to get Storm over this ditch. I think we should make camp and set off again at first light."

"Good idea," Elenna said, but then a sudden, distant shout made her heart clench. "That sounds like Tom," she gasped.

"He might be in trouble," Daltec said. "Let's hurry!" The young wizard half-climbed, half-skidded down the bank, landing heavily in the mud at the bottom. Still holding Storm's reins, Elenna eased herself downwards slowly, but when Storm reached the edge of the bank, he shook his head and let out a snort.

"Come on," Elenna said softly. Storm whickered, the whites of his eyes showing clearly in the low light. Elenna tugged at his reins gently. "You can do it," she said. Storm turned until he was almost side-on to the ditch and tentatively stepped over the edge.

"Good boy!" Elenna said, lowering herself further down the bank. The stallion followed her, his big hooves sinking deep into the waterlogged mud. Then suddenly, with a terrified scream that made Elenna's heart lurch, Storm slipped. Elenna threw herself out of the stallion's path as

he tumbled, rolling sideways, his hooves flailing in the air. He crashed down into the trench, then struggled in the mud, trying to stand, his nostrils flaring and his eyes wild. Elenna slipped and skidded to his side.

"Easy, Storm," she said, gathering the horse's reins. Daltec joined her. Together, ankle-deep in mud, they somehow managed to pull the terrified stallion to his feet.

"Nearly there," Elenna said softly as she led Storm, who was snorting and puffing, towards the far bank. Then she froze, as a strange vibration ran up through the mud into her legs. She could hear a distant rumbling sound. Storm's head went up, and he gave an anxious whicker.

"What is that?" Daltec asked, his eyes wide as he gazed about. Then his mouth dropped open, and he pointed a shaking finger past Elenna. "We have to get out!" he cried.

Elenna turned to see a vast boulder crashing towards them, rolling along the gully, filling it entirely from one edge to the other. *No!* She quickly tugged Storm to the far side of the gully. Daltec was already climbing. Elenna scrambled up the muddy bank behind him, pulling Storm's reins, forcing the panicked horse to follow her. Planting his hooves in the slippery mud, Storm clambered upwards, his eyes rolling with terror as the rumbling, crashing sound grew louder. As they neared the top of the bank, Elenna stole a glance

over her shoulder. Dread seared through her as she saw the boulder hurtling closer. *It's moving so fast!*

"Here!" Daltec called, putting out a hand to help her. Elenna took it, holding Storm's reins in her other hand. But as she reached the bank, the stallion slipped, tearing the leather straps from her grip. With a scream of terror, Storm tumbled back into the mud.

Horror squeezed Elenna's heart.

"He'll be crushed!" Daltec said.

"No!" Elenna told him. "Storm! To me!" The horse started to scramble up the slope once more. By now, the rumbling was almost deafening, and a vile, musty stench filled the air.

Glancing sideways, Elenna saw the boulder thundering close, filling her vision, almost on top of Storm.

"Now!" she cried to Daltec as Storm's head came within reach. She and the wizard both made a grab for his bridle, caught hold of it, and heaved with all the strength they could muster.

In a blur of flailing hooves and flying mud, Storm scrambled out of the ditch, sending Elenna and Daltec toppling backwards. In what felt like the same heartbeat, the huge boulder rumbled past, and in another instant, it was gone, disappearing into the darkness of the forest.

Elenna sat dazed, blinking for a

moment, her mind reeling. As the boulder had passed, she thought she had made out the pattern of interlocking armoured plates all over it. And she was almost sure she had caught a glimpse of a dark, shining eye.

"What was that thing?" she asked, panting.

Daltec glanced along the ditch, then looked back at her, his face pale in the darkness. He swallowed hard. When he finally spoke, there was a quiver in his voice. "I believe it may have been a Beast..."

TRAPPED IN THE TREETOPS

Strong, leathery hands swung Tom upwards by his arms through scratching branches, to where more green, monkey-like folk gripped his ankles. Dark foliage whipped past him as he flipped upside down, only to feel his arms seized tightly once again. His head spun as he was tossed from one hairy creature to another, flipping over and over, glossy leaves speeding past and the crack and snap of branches loud in his ears. From up ahead he could hear Ria shrieking curses, and he caught the occasional glimpse of her furious face as she too was tossed through the trees by the strange monkey people.

"Put me down or I'll pummel the lot of you!" Tom cried.

"As you wish," a female voice said from close above him. A moment later, the hands gripping his shoulders and legs all let go at once. His stomach lurched as he fell, crashing through the branches. *I should have kept my mouth shut*, he thought, tensing his muscles, bracing himself for a hard impact on the forest floor. But instead, he landed on something soft and springy high in the canopy. With a cry of surprise, Ria came down beside him, bounced once, then scrambled up to a sitting position. Tom glanced about to see they had fallen into a huge, moss-lined nest woven from branches.

Tom peered further into the shadowy treetops and made out half a dozen stocky, green monkey-folk gazing back at him. Now he could see them properly, he noticed that their tufty, grey-green fur matched the colour of the tree moss. Although they were short, all had broad chests

and sinewy, muscular arms and legs. Some were very small – children, perhaps; others had deep creases in the leathery skin of their faces, and gnarly cracked nails on their fingers and toes. All watched him and Ria

intently, their dark eyes shining in the low light.

"What are you waiting for?" Ria hissed at Tom, getting to her feet. "Deal with them."

Tom snatched his sword from his

belt and brandished it.

"Let us go now, or you'll be sorry!" Tom snarled. The smaller monkey-folk shrank away from him with gasps of alarm. But one of the nearest creatures, broad and barrel-chested, with smooth skin and bright eyes, sent a vine whip lashing towards him. Before Tom could react, the whip wrapped about his sword and snatched it from his grip.

"Useless!" Ria snarled. "Fine...I'll do it myself." Ria lifted her hands, conjuring two balls of purple fire. But more whips cracked out from the tree's foliage and caught hold of her wrists, pulling her arms out straight either side of her.

"Let me go!" Ria cried, the purple magic in her hands fizzling away as she struggled against her bonds.

One of the wrinkled, older-looking monkey people stepped forwards and made a quick bow, then stood watching them with keen, dark eyes.

"My name is Rani," the creature said, in a stern female voice. "We do not wish to fight you."

"Then why did you kidnap us?" Ria growled through clenched teeth, still wrenching at the vines gripping her arms.

"Our intention was not to kidnap you, but to rescue you," Rani said. "It is not safe to walk the forest floor at night when the Beast is active. You would not have lasted long."

"We're here to defeat the Beast, not hide from it," Tom cried. "Let us go!"

The monkey-folk, crowded close behind Rani, exchanged quick glances. Then one started to snigger. Soon, all were hooting with laughter. Only Rani stood silent, her expression grave as she held Tom's eyes.

"What?" Tom demanded.

Rani shook her head, almost pityingly. "You may as well say you are going to catch the moon in a net," she told Tom. "You cannot defeat Morax. You can only hope to avoid him."

As the monkey-creatures sniggered and tittered, and Rani gazed sorrowfully at him, Tom felt as if his blood might boil. "I am Master of the Beasts!" he cried. "Every Beast I have met, I have vanquished! Do you doubt my strength and courage?"

Rani frowned, but something about the kindly expression in her eyes made Tom angrier than ever. "I do not doubt your courage," she said, "but you have not met Morax. If you had, you would not say such things."

"I'll make up my own mind," Tom said. "Give me back my sword."

Rani shook her head. "You will bring trouble to us all. Sleep now. We will let you go at dawn." Rani turned and made a signal to the forest creatures behind her. The two monkey-like folk holding the vine whips coiled about Ria's arms tied them to a low branch, so Ria could lie down. A few others stayed to stand guard over Tom and Ria, but most swung on to mossy nests half-hidden among the branches and huddled in groups, settling down for the night. The moon pierced through the leaves, casting dappled shadows around Tom and Ria, and with the sun gone, the cold night air felt keen and sharp. Ria shivered and drew her cloak close about her.

"It's all right for them, all snuggled together and covered in fur," she said. "We'll freeze up here before morning."

"I don't intend to wait for morning," Tom said.

"So, what are you going to do?" Ria asked. "Jump?"

"No. I'm going to heat things up a bit around here," Tom said. He crouched with his back to their guards and picked up a pair of sticks. Then, heaping dry moss around one of the sticks, he rested the other on top of it and started rolling it quickly between his hands. Before long, a thin trail of smoke rose from his kindling. Tom blew gently, and the kindling glimmered orange. With another breath, it flared into bright flame. Tom fed more moss into the blaze, feeling a wild excitement stir inside him as his little fire spread,

hungrily consuming the kindling and growing by the moment.

"What have you done?" a youngish

voice suddenly cried from nearby. Tom turned to see a forest creature shoot to his feet, his eyes wide with terror as flames licked high, making a curtain of flickering orange between them.

"You might all be afraid of the Beast," Tom said, "but I'm not. I'm going to lure it here, and then I'm going to fight!"

DANGER
1

FOREST FIRE

Elenna led Storm as she and Daltec picked their way through the gloomy forest, following the line of Tom's compass as closely as they could. Though the stallion had recovered well from his fall, the moss and tangled vines hanging from above meant it was quicker to walk than ride. Elenna strained her ears, listening for any sign that Tom might be close. But all she could hear was their own footsteps. *I hope he's all right*, she thought. *He has to be! We've come through worse than this*.

They soon reached a clearing in the forest, where the moon shone brightly, revealing the splintered remains of fallen trees. Between the broken trunks, Elenna spotted what looked like pieces of trelliswork woven from sticks and caulked with moss and mud.

As Elenna led Storm into the clearing, she saw a carved wooden bowl on the floor, and the remains of a mossy nest bed still clinging to the branches of one of the felled trees.

Daltec stooped and picked up a wooden spoon. Even in the low light, Elenna could see it was beautifully crafted. "This must have been made by the people who live in the forest," Daltec said.

"Or lived..." Elenna said. Then she suddenly tensed all over, a sick, scared feeling coiled in the pit of her stomach and her heart beating fast. It took her a moment to register why. Storm stamped and snorted, tossing his head. *Smoke!* The smell was faint, but unmistakable. Not the clean, sweet smoke of seasoned wood burning, but the choking green smoke of living trees.

"There's a forest fire," Elenna said

to Daltec, her voice quivering.

Daltec nodded. "The smoke is coming from up ahead, where the compass is pointing. We should press on. Tom could be in danger." Then he looked at her, concerned. "Do you think you'll be all right?"

Elenna shivered, but then squared her shoulders, and nodded. "I lost my parents in a forest fire," she said. "I'm not going to lose Tom that way, too."

They pushed through the jungle as quickly as they could, the smoke thickening as they went. Before long, they saw what looked like a wall of trees, planted close together, looming in the darkness ahead.

When they reached it, Elenna ran her eyes up the huge trunks to see they were branchless and sharpened at the top. *A stockade*, she realised. But now many of the massive stakes leaned against each other at odd angles, while others lay splintered. Deep gouges and drag marks in the damp earth sent a cold finger of dread down Elenna's spine. They looked a lot like enormous claw prints.

"What do you think?" she asked Daltec. "It's like someone built a fence to keep something in."

"Or to keep something *out*..." Daltec said, gazing around the destruction. "And it would have to be something huge."

"That boulder-Beast thing?" Elenna said.

"I'm beginning to think anything is possible," Daltec answered.

They left the wreckage of the stockade behind and pressed further into the jungle. The smoke seemed to thicken with each step, making Elenna's eyes smart and her throat feel raw. She lifted her sleeve to cover her nose and mouth. Daltec did the same. Storm let out anxious snorts and whickers.

"I know, Storm," Elenna told the stallion, "but we can't give up searching until we've found Tom." At the mention of Tom's name, Storm lifted his head and gave it a shake, then picked up his pace, almost as if he had understood.

Soon, Elenna could hear the rustle of leaves and branches above, mingled with the distant crackle of flames. An orange glow smouldered in the darkness ahead and smoke billowed thick all around them. She looked up to see fleeting shadows high in the canopy. *Some sort of animal escaping the fire...* Suddenly, a twig cracked right above her head, followed by a squeal, and Elenna spotted one of the shadowy creatures plummeting towards her. She threw out her hands and snatched the falling bundle from the air.

"Goodness!" Daltec asked. "What's that?" Elenna looked at the furry creature in her arms, and her mouth dropped open in amazement. A

small green monkey with a heart-shaped face started back at her, its eyes huge and round.

"Give me my baby!" an angry voice snapped, and a larger version of the tiny creature clambered down a tree trunk to stand before Elenna, baring its yellow teeth in a snarl. The baby in Elenna's hands squirmed and leapt, landing at its mother's shoulder, then burying its face in her fur.

"I don't know why you strange folk have come here," the child's mother said, frowning crossly, "but you've brought nothing but trouble. You're not welcome!"

"I'm looking for my friend," Elenna said. "His name's Tom."

The forest woman's fur bristled, and she shook her head. "If you're friends with that young villain, you are no friend of ours," she said, and as she spoke, Elenna felt the ground beneath her feet begin to shake, violently. "Now run, if you've any sense at all," the monkey woman added. "Morax is here." Then she turned and leapt on to a tree trunk, her baby staring back over her shoulder until they vanished out of sight.

Storm let out a frightened neigh. Daltec grabbed Elenna's shoulder, pointing. The earth before them had begun to bulge, huge cracks spreading over the surface. Mud fell away, crumbling into rivulets that ran down the sides of the bulge. Elenna and Daltec backed away hurriedly, while Storm turned and fled into the darkness of the

forest. The trees either side of the giant bulge creaked and groaned, starting to list and lean. Then, with a deafening roar, they toppled, their pale roots lifting clear of the ground as something else poked up from the dark earth. A vast scaled snout, long and narrow, lined with needle-sharp teeth. Elenna quickly strung an arrow to her bow and took aim, waiting for the Beast to emerge.

I've never faced a Beast without Tom, she thought. *I wish he were here with me now...*

A CHINK IN THE ARMOUR

Tom watched from a branch high in the canopy as the flames of his fire took hold, leaping from tree to tree, making the sap crack and pop. *It didn't take long for those cowardly monkeys to flee*, he thought. He could hear them now, hooting and shrieking as they clambered through the treetops. As soon as his guards had left, Tom had retrieved his sword, and cut Ria's bonds. Then they had climbed to a better vantage point, clear of the smoke and flames.

"Morax is coming!" Ria said, pointing through the branches towards a huge bulge forming on the forest floor. Tom felt a shudder run through the wood beneath his feet. With a splintering crash, the trees either side of the mound toppled, and the earth broke open, revealing a long slender snout lined with teeth. Sharp claws followed, shoving the earth aside, making way for an armoured head with small, beady eyes. As the Beast clambered from the earth, Tom saw that his vast body was covered all over with interlocking plates.

Morax's nose twitched, as if sniffing for prey, and his round eyes scanned the trees, fixing on the fleeing monkey people. With a hungry grunt, like a pig scenting truffles, the Beast tucked his head down. Morax's armoured plates slid easily over each other until he looked more like a boulder than a Beast. Suddenly, with a flick of his tail, Morax started to roll.

CRASH! Morax smashed into a nearby tree, toppling it. The few monkey creatures still clinging to

the branches screamed in terror and leapt to the ground, scattering and racing for cover. The Beast rolled about, smashing through blazing bushes, crushing anything in his path.

Tom grinned and tightened his grip on his sword, watching as Morax unrolled once more. The Beast turned, his pink snout twitching and his tiny orange eyes swivelling this way and that.

"This Beast is truly a worthy adversary!" Tom said to Ria at his side. "Once I've killed it, I'll be the greatest warrior ever!"

"Just make sure you do kill it!" Ria said. Tom thought he could detect a note of fear in her voice. He turned to see her face pale in the flickering light, and her eyes glinting.

"Don't worry," he told her. "You stay here. I'll handle this!"

"That is exactly what I intend to do," Ria said. But at that moment, the Beast turned and looked directly up at them. Tom felt a tingle of warmth from the red jewel in his belt as he locked eyes with the creature.

I know you! the Beast's voice bellowed in Tom's mind. *I recognise a descendant of Tanner when I see one. I will crush you like an ant and feast on your remains!* Then the Beast ducked his head and rolled towards Tom and Ria's tree. *BOOF!* Tom felt the wood he clung to judder, and almost lost his grip.

Ria fell, but managed to catch the branch and pull herself back up.

"I thought you were going to fight that thing!" she shrieked. "Go!"

Tom started to clamber down the tree, lowering himself from branch to branch. The Beast rolled back a little way, then came straight in for another strike. Tom gripped tight to the trunk. *CRASH!* He managed to keep his footing, but his stomach lurched as he felt the trunk itself list towards the forest floor. The Beast rolled back again. Tom knew that one more hit would send the tree toppling with Ria still clinging to her branch. *I have to protect her… I have to kill the Beast!*

Tom measured the distance to the ground with his eyes and jumped. He landed in a crouch and leapt up, brandishing his sword.

Morax had uncoiled and stood motionless, his beady eyes fixed on Tom. Beyond the Beast, Tom could see flames leaping high. He could feel the scalding heat of the fire on his skin. But heedless of the flames, the Beast stomped towards him, his pointed teeth glinting in the firelight. A long blue tongue, muscular and quick, flicked from between Morax's jaws. Black liquid dripped from its tip, hissing and smoking as it hit the ground.

Poison! Tom realised. *No matter.*

I am more than a match for you! He grinned and lifted his sword, ready to fight. But at that moment, an arrow whizzed through the air and struck Morax on the side, skittering off his armoured shell. The Beast turned as Elenna leapt from the blazing forest, her face smudged with soot, and another arrow already fitted to her bow.

Tom scowled at her. "Leave the fighting to the real hero!" he told her. Then he charged headlong towards the Beast, a fierce hunger for battle swelling inside him. He swung his sword, aiming for Morax's pink snout, but at the same moment, the Beast flicked its blackened tongue towards him. "OOF!" The impact was like the lash of a giant whip, sending Tom flying. He landed on his side, his head slamming into something hard, making blinding pain flare inside his skull.

Tom shook his head to clear the dizziness and saw a movement nearby. A small, furry ape-child stared back at him from inside a bush, its teeth bared with fear. The tiny creature's dark, shining eyes flicked to the sword in Tom's hand, then back to his face, filled with terror. Then the child leapt from the bush and ran…right into the path of Morax. The monkey-child stopped, frozen with horror, staring up at the Beast, whose eyes flashed hungrily.

Then Morax ducked his head and started to roll.

Tom a felt a sharp catching

sensation in his chest – a strange, squeezing pain at the sight of the Beast bearing down on the defenceless creature. Before he could think or understand his own actions, he found himself up and running,

pounding over the forest floor towards the small green child.

"What are you doing?" Ria screamed from above him. But Tom couldn't answer. He threw himself down over the little green bundle, shielding the child's body with his own as the Beast's massive bulk crashed towards them. Too late to move, Tom tucked his head down, braced his muscles and waited, ready for death.

DANGER
1

AN UNBREAKABLE BOND

Horror clutched at Elenna's chest as she saw Tom crouch low over the tiny green creature, while the Beast thundered towards them. *They'll be crushed!* she realised. Morax's massive bulk soon blocked her view of Tom and the child. Elenna could hardly bear to watch, but sick terror kept her frozen, unable to look away. Suddenly, with a furious scream, a dark shape burst from between two blazing trees. *Storm!* she realised, as the stallion reared and slammed his hooves hard into

Morax's body, knocking the Beast off course.

Tom started to rise, one arm still cradling the tiny forest creature. Tears sprang to Elenna's eyes as she saw him glance down at the small green monkey. *Tom put his own life in danger to save that child!* she realised. Tom frowned, as if confused, then let the little monkey go.

"Thank you!" the small creature said, and with a terrified glance at the flames all around them, it scurried away.

Storm lowered his head and whickered at Tom. As Tom gazed back at his horse, Elenna saw his confused expression turn to wonder. He put out a hand, as if to stroke the stallion's nose. But then Elenna heard a crack, coupled with a shriek of alarm, that snatched Tom's attention from his horse. Elenna turned to see Ria tumble from a split and smouldering tree branch.

The witch hit the ground and staggered to her feet. And at the same moment, Morax appeared behind her, his gold eyes bright with triumph. "Look out!" Tom cried, as the Beast's blue tongue flicked out towards the witch. Ria spun to face her attacker, just as a green whip cracked through the air, coiling around the Beast's snout and yanking it sideways.

Elenna looked into the dancing shadows between two trees to see Daltec holding the other end of the whip, with Rani at his side. *He must have gone for help while I was watching Tom!*

"Attack!" Rani cried. More monkey-people dropped to the ground, and more whips lashed out to snag Morax's jaws and fasten them shut, so that his blue tongue hung limp and his eyes bulged with hatred.

Morax bucked and reared up on to his hind legs, dragging the monkey-folk across the forest floor by the whips in their hands. Seeing the Beast's exposed underbelly, leathery and soft with no armour at all, Elenna's hands flew to her bow. She nocked an arrow and took aim. But, letting out a strangled, throaty roar, Morax shook his head wildly, throwing his captors aside. With the monkey-people in her way, Elenna couldn't get a clear shot. Morax curled into a ball and rolled straight towards her. Panic surged through Elenna's veins. She let her arrow fly, but watched it ping harmlessly off Morax's hide as she dived out of the monster's path.

Elenna shrank back as Morax thundered past her, so close she felt a rush of air. She could almost have reached out to touch his scales. Scrambling to her feet, she saw the Beast smash into a mighty tree, which was already engulfed in flames. With a hideous groan, the tree toppled and fell right on top of the Beast, scattering burning twigs and branches all around him. Elenna scrambled away from the burning debris and stared at the pyre-like blaze before her. The fire was so intense, she couldn't see Morax at all.

Is the Beast dead?

THE FINAL BEAST

His chest swelling with fury, Tom stormed through the chaos of smoke and flames, barging past cowering monkey-people to where Elenna stood staring, mouth open, at the blazing remains of the fallen tree.

"You fool!" he shouted at her. "That was the perfect opportunity for a killing shot and you missed!"

"But...surely it's dead?" Elenna stammered.

"No!" Tom cried. "I can feel its presence as strongly as ever." He turned towards the flaming pyre that hid the Beast. He could already see a great dark shape stirring within. "See!" he said, pointing. At that moment, the Beast burst from the flames, snout twitching and eyes filled with rage as they swivelled this way and that, looking for prey. Morax's armoured hide was black with soot, but otherwise, he seemed unharmed.

"Morax is formidable," Tom heard Daltec say from behind him. He turned to see the snivelling young

wizard emerge from the flickering shadows of the forest. "I don't know how we're going to defeat him!" Daltec went on. "He can roll up whenever he needs to. If fire and a falling tree can't harm him, what chance does a human weapon have? Maybe if we work together– "

Tom had heard enough. "Leave it to a Master of the Beasts," he snapped, cutting Daltec short. Then he turned back towards the huge bulk of the Beast, now stalking towards them. *I know I can defeat Morax*, he told himself. *I can defeat any Beast!* Then suddenly, looking at the blackened armour plates that covered Morax's body, Tom had an idea.

"What if I somehow stopped the Beast rolling up?" he said, almost to himself. He heard a disdainful snort, and glanced over to see Ria hobbling towards them, covered in soot and scratches, her face twisted with scorn.

"What are you going to do? Tickle its tummy?" she spat. "You lot are all as pathetic as each other."

Tom glared at the witch, a terrible fury growing inside him. *She doesn't believe I can do it, either... Well, I'll show her!*

"I think what we need is a distraction," Tom said, and he grabbed Ria by her shoulders. Her eyes went wide and she opened her mouth to speak, but Tom dragged her into the path of Morax, then shoved her towards the enormous Beast.

"What are you doing?" Ria cried. She landed on her hands and knees and struggled to her feet, just as the Beast's orange eyes fixed on her. Tom smiled as Morax's blue tongue twitched from between his lips as if tasting the air. *This might just work...*

Calling on the power of his magic boots, Tom bent his knees and leapt. With a rush of speed, he soared over Ria's head and landed squarely on the Beast's armoured back. Letting his shield drop to his arm, Tom drove it hard down between two scales. As he jammed the shield in place, Tom felt the Beast's body stiffen beneath him. *Yes!* Morax lifted his snout and let out a throaty, anguished growl. Tom vaulted lightly back to the ground and drew his sword.

"Come on, then," he called to the Beast. "Fight me!"

The Beast started to writhe, shaking his head back and forth, trying to free Tom's shield. Ria scrambled away as Morax let out a furious roar. Then, his eyes bulging with fury, the Beast tucked his head down, as if trying to roll into a ball. And stopped. Morax tried ducking his head at a different angle. But again, Tom's shield prevented the smooth scales from sliding over each other. *Ha ha! It worked!* Tom grinned as the Beast reared up and glared back at him, eyes burning with hate as his voice roared in Tom's mind:

Child of Tanner's blood, now you will die... I will crush you... I will squash you flat... I will pulverise every bone in your body!

Tightening his grip on his sword,

Tom held the Beast's gaze. Morax lumbered forwards, unsteady on his hind feet as if the shield in his scales unbalanced him, his front claws extended. *Now's my chance!* Focussing on the Beast's soft underbelly, Tom lunged, swinging his sword. But at the same moment, Morax's blue tongue flickered from between his lips. It struck Tom hard in the chest. Tom flew through the air and landed on his back, all the air thrust from his lungs at once. He blinked to clear his vision and looked up to see the Beast looming over him – a towering mass of solid armoured flesh. Tom's mouth went dry and his chest tightened with fear.

The Beast bared his pointed teeth. *Now you die!*

Tom braced himself and closed his eyes, his heart hammering in his chest and all his nerves firing. *This is it...I'm going to be crushed!*

But then he heard the twang of an arrow, followed by a mighty, bellowing cry. He opened his eyes to see the Beast stagger sideways, a shaft protruding from the leathery hide of his belly.

Tom glanced through the flickering shadows to see Elenna lowering her bow. *She saved my life…* As Tom staggered up, the Beast started to shake, his whole vast body shuddering so violently that his armoured plates clattered together. Then, with a thunderous rattling crash, like a blast of mighty hailstones, Morax vanished in a cloud of thick black smoke.

Through the smoke, Tom saw a single, sharp yellow tooth drop to the forest floor along with his shield. *The token!* Tom lunged for it. But his hand met Elenna's as she too made a grab for the tooth. At the same moment, Daltec let out a cry of pain from behind Elenna. Tom looked up to see the wizard pinned to the ground beneath a fallen smouldering branch.

"You'd better help your friend," Tom told Elenna, holding her gaze. He could see from her anguished expression that she was torn. But finally, she glanced over her shoulder and started to rise. Tom snatched the tooth from her hand and ran.

Ria leapt from the shadows to meet him, smiling. "So, you've finally developed a backbone," she said, her eyes bright with mischief. "Are you ready to meet the final Beast of Pyloris?"

Tom frowned. "Surely that was the last of Krokol's children?" he said.

Ria's smile spread into a wide, evil grin. "That's right. There were three children. Now it's time to resurrect Krokol himself – a Beast so terrible, even Tanner couldn't beat him."

Ria whistled for her winged stallion, which swooped from the smoke-filled sky to land before them, snorting and eyeing the flames anxiously.

"Come on!" Ria said, leaping on to her stallion's back. Tom swung up behind her. Then he took one last look over his shoulder at where Elenna and a group of the green monkey-folk were struggling to free

Daltec. He spotted other monkey-people among the trees carrying axes, while still more had buckets of water and were trying to tackle the

fire. Tom felt a strange pang in his chest. *Elenna is brave...she saved my life. Maybe I should help her.*

But, before he could move, Ria drove her heels hard into her horse's sides. With a flap of its mighty wings, the stallion carried them into the sky.

As Tom glanced back at the flaming forest, getting further away by the moment, he could see small green folk racing around, cutting down trees, making a firebreak. Others had formed a chain from a boggy pool to the fire and were filling buckets. Daltec was on his feet now, pointing his finger, giving instructions. Only Elenna stood still, gazing up at the sky, her eyes filled with sorrow. *She's looking at me...* Tom felt something stir in his chest. A painful yearning. He turned away to stare ahead, swallowing the strange ache, and instead focussed on the familiar mix of excitement and dread growing inside him.

Time to face a true adversary, he told himself. *Time to kill the final Beast!*

THE END

CONGRATULATIONS, YOU HAVE COMPLETED THIS QUEST!

At the end of each chapter you were awarded a special gold coin. The QUEST in this book was worth an amazing 8 coins.

Look at the Beast Quest totem picture opposite to see how far you've come in your journey to become

MASTER OF THE BEASTS.

The more books you read, the more coins you will collect!

Do you want your own Beast Quest Totem?

1. Cut out and collect the coin below
2. Go to the Beast Quest website
3. Download and print out your totem
4. Add your coin to the totem

www.beastquest.co.uk

READ THE BOOKS, COLLECT THE COINS!

EARN COINS FOR EVERY CHAPTER YOU READ!

550+ COINS
MASTER OF THE BEASTS

410 COINS
HERO

350 COINS
WARRIOR

230 COINS
KNIGHT

180 COINS
SQUIRE

44 COINS
PAGE

8 COINS
APPRENTICE

550+
515
480
445
410
395
380
365
350
320
290
260
230
217
206
191
180
146
112
78
44
30
19
8

Don't miss the next Beast Quest adventure. Read on for a sneak peek...

"There it is!" cried Daltec. "The Great Palace of Pyloris!"

"Or what's left of it," muttered Elenna.

The journey from the forest of Morax had been long and slow, across sweeping plains, but Elenna resisted the urge to rest. A wide stone path stretched ahead, leading straight through overgrown gardens to the palace.

Once, the Great Palace of Pyloris must have been white. But now the stones were dirty and crumbling, and the high walls were covered in creeping green vines. The great golden domes on each tower had turned dull with neglect.

Under the grey sky, the air was chill. Elenna couldn't help shivering. *It's so quiet here...*

"It looks completely abandoned," said Daltec.

Elenna shook her head. "I'm not so sure." She unhooked the compass from her belt and checked the black needle, which wobbled to aim right at the palace. The needle was made from the same metal as Tom's armour, now under an Evil enchantment, and it always pointed straight to him. "Tom's in there," she said. "So we'd better take a closer

look."

We've got to find him, Elenna reminded herself.

As they passed a pair of dried-up old fountains, Elenna couldn't shake off an uneasy feeling. There was no sign of life here. Not even a twittering of birdsong.

Ahead, a row of stone soldiers stood guard on either side of the path, like sentries on duty. Their faces were worn away by time, and most of their spears had broken off entirely.

Daltec was panting, struggling to keep up. "Be careful!" he said. "We don't know what might be waiting for us in there."

Look out for
KROKOL, THE FATHER OF FEAR
to find out what happens next...

READ ALL THE BOOKS IN SERIES 24:

BLOOD OF THE BEAST!

Meet three new heroes with the power to tame the Beasts!

Amy, Charlie and Sam – three children from our world – are about to discover the powerful legacy that binds them together.

They are descendants of the *Guardians of Avantia*, an elite group of heroes trained by Tom himself.

Now the time has come for a new generation to unlock the power of the Beasts and fulfil their destiny.

Read on for a sneak peek at how the Guardians first left Avantia by magic…

Karita of Banquise gazed in awe at Tom, Avantia's mighty, bearded Master of the Beasts.

Under his leadership, she and her companions would today face their greatest challenge.

Tom pointed towards the brooding Gorgonian castle. "We must recover the chest of Beast Eggs Malvel stole," he reminded them. His fierce blue eyes moved from Karita to the others. Dell of Stonewin, whose bloodline connected him to Beasts of Fire; Fern of Errinel, linked to Storm Beasts; Gustus of Colton, bonded with Water Beasts.

"Malvel will be expecting an attack," Tom said. "His power is lessened, but he is still formidable." His eyes locked on Karita. "Stealth will be our greatest ally."

Karita felt as though her whole life had been a preparation for this moment. Countless hours spent studying the ancient tomes, day after day of gruelling combat training, months learning how to influence the will of Stealth Beasts and control the powers that filled the Arcane Band at her wrist.

But was she ready?

She gazed into Tom's face, and her doubts faded.

Yes!

A low rumble came from the

castle. Flashes of green lightning shot from the clouds as a swarm of screeching creatures erupted from the battlements.

Karita shuddered as Malvel's hideous minions streaked through the sky. They were man-sized, with white hides, limbs tipped with hooked claws and gaping jaws lined with sharp teeth. Their leathery wings cracked like whips.

"Karrakhs!" muttered Tom. "Karita – go!"

She nodded and slipped away behind jagged rocks. She turned to see the swarm of foul creatures engulf her companions. Tom's sword flashed. Howls rang out from the Karrakhs. The Guardians were using their Arcane Bands to form weapons that spun and slashed!

Karita raced for the castle, keeping low behind the ridge of rocks. Reaching the walls, she climbed up a gnarled vine and found a narrow window to crawl through. She looked back again. Tom and the Guardians had battled their way through the castle gates.

Well fought!

She dropped into a room and crept to the door. Torches burned in the corridor, casting shadows. The castle was silent, but Karita felt a growing dread as she slipped along the walls.

She knew where the chest of Beast eggs was hidden. But would Malvel allow her to get to them?

She came to a circular room, and saw the chest standing by the wall. Her heart hammering, Karita opened the lid and gazed down at the eggs. They were different sizes, shapes and colours. One slipped from the pile and she caught it in her gloved hand. It was pale blue, about the size of a goose egg. Acting on instinct, she slipped it inside her breastplate.

Crash!

She spun around. Malvel stood against the room's closed door.

"Did you really think you could enter my domain unseen?" he snarled, a green glow igniting in his palm. His voice was weaker than she'd imagined. "I *wanted* you to come here. After all, only a Guardian can hatch a Beast Egg."

Karita swallowed hard, seeking a way to escape.

"You and your friends will hatch these Beasts and I will drink in their power," growled the wizard. "I will become mighty again and Avantia will bow before me!"

"I'm not afraid of you!" Karita shouted.

A ball of green fire exploded from Malvel's hand. Karita dived aside, seared by the heat.

She leaped up, thrusting her right arm towards the wizard. The Arcane Band began to form a weapon, but another blast of fire sent her sliding across the floor.

Malvel loomed over her, both hands

burning green. Before he could strike, the door burst open and Tom and the Guardians rushed into the room.

"No!" roared Malvel. "Where are my Karrakhs?"

"Defeated!" shouted Tom, whirling his sword to deflect Malvel's green flames. "Guardians! Take the eggs!"

Fern dived for the chest, but a blast from the wizard knocked her over.

"The eggs are mine!" howled Malvel. He traced a large circle of fire in the air. There was a blast of hot wind as the flaming hoop crackled and spat.

Malvel snatched up the chest and turned to the heart of the fiery circle.

"He's opened a portal!" shouted

Tom. "Stop him!"

Gustus ran at the wizard and wrested the chest from his grip. Roaring in anger, Malvel launched a fireball, but Fern managed to shove Gustus out of its path. But the force of her push knocked Gustus into the portal. With a stifled cry, he and the chest of eggs were gone.

"No!" Fern shouted, diving in after him. With a shout, Dell ran after her.

"Wait!" shouted Tom.

"It's our duty to protect the eggs!" Dell called back as he disappeared into the swirling portal.

Malvel sprang forward, but Tom bounded in front of him, holding him back with his spinning blade as the wizard hurled magical fireballs.

Karita saw the walls of the portal writhing and distorting. Malvel's fireballs were making it unstable. At any moment it might vanish!

Tom was knocked back by a torrent of green fire as the wizard turned and leaped into the portal. Karita flung herself after him.

"No! Karita!" The last thing she heard was Tom's voice. "The portal is in flux! You could be sent anywhere!"

And then there was nothing but a rushing wind and howling darkness, as she plunged into the unknown.

Look out for
Beast Quest: New Blood
to find out what happens next!

THEIR GIFTS MAKE THEM DIFFERENT
NICE HANDS!
FREAK!

BUT WHEN DANGER COMES...
CRACK!
RUMBLE!

SCREEECH!

...A HERO IS BORN

OTHERS WITH GIFTS WILL SEEK THEM OUT...

...AND SHOW THEM THEIR DESTINY.
EVER HEARD OF HERO ACADEMY?

OUT NOW!

ADAM BLADE
TEAM HERO
BATTLE FOR THE SHADOW SWORD

ADAM BLADE
TEAM HERO
ATTACK OF THE BAT ARMY

ADAM BLADE
TEAM HERO
REPTILE REAWAKENED

ADAM BLADE
TEAM HERO
THE SKELETON WARRIOR